No One Walks on
My Father's Moon

Story by
Chara M. Curtis

Illustrations by
Rebecca Hyland

Voyage Publishing

No One Walks on
My Father's
Moon

Story by Chara M. Curtis

Illustrations by Rebecca Hyland

Voyage Publishing • Anacortes, Washington USA

There once was a boy who was eager to learn all this great world could teach him. He lived with his hard-working father outside a small village where donkeys and horsecarts carried vegetables to market and modern inventions were yet a future away. The boy's father had never gone to school, having learned all he knew from his father and grandfather. Besides teaching him to work, they had taught him to read the Qur'an, the Holy Book of Islam. This was the only book the boy's father ever read, because it was the only book he trusted to be true.

One day the boy sent dust clouds swirling behind him as he raced home after school. "Oh, Father!" the boy said, nearly out of breath. "Wait till you hear. A great thing has happened before it could even be imagined!"

"What are you talking about?" his father asked. "Hurry and tell me, for we have much to do before the sun goes to sleep."

"The Americans, Father. They sent an airship far into the sky. When it landed, a man walked on the moon."

This he said, for this is what he had learned.

His father's face turned suddenly to stone. "How dare you lie to me!" he said. "Does your tongue wag so that the devil can visit my ears? No one can walk on the face of God's shining light! No one and nothing, not ever! Not only are you sinful in telling a lie, your falsehood is a mockery to the wonder of God's creation. You must apologize to me this very minute, and in the next you must seek Allah's forgiveness."

This he said, for this is what he believed.

"But, Father, I am not lying. It is true!" the boy insisted. "My teacher told us. The Americans even showed pictures on their television."

The old man's hands shook with rage. "You are a disgrace!" he said. "More lies will not make your first lie true. You bring shame upon this house and fear into my heart. You must take back your sinful words."

"But, Father, I swear I am telling the truth. A man walked on the moon. You must believe me. I can prove it!"

The old man could not bear to hear any more. He picked up a stick and waved it toward the sky. "I pray to God my son will see the error of his ways," he said. And with that, he grabbed the boy and beat him until he was too weak to utter a cry. Though mean and cruel, this is what the father did, for in this way was he punished when he was yet a son.

When it was over, the man held out his hand for his son to kiss, as was the custom in which a father received obedience and respect. But the beating had hurt the boy's heart even more than it had hurt his body, and so his lips fell cold and numb against his father's hand, the warm blood of love no longer flowing through his veins.

The next day the boy did not return to school. Nor the day after, nor the day after that. When at last he took his seat in the classroom, his teacher wanted to know the reason for his absence.

"My father says it is not possible for a man to walk on the moon, which is the face of God's holy light. He says it is a sin to speak of such things, and now I will never be allowed to see the gates of heaven."

The teacher looked with love into the boy's tear-filled eyes. "I am sorry for your pain," he said. "What else did your father say?"

"Nothing," the boy replied. "He punished me with a beating and told me I must pray. But when I prayed, I told God a terrible thing. I told Him I hate my father. I know it is a sin, but it is true. Maybe it would be better for me if I learned to lie."

The teacher left the boy alone to cry his tears, for this is what a hurting child must do if he is to heal.

After a while the boy raised his hand, asking, "Teacher, is it possible there is more than one moon?"

His teacher was surprised to hear such a question. Surely the answer was obvious. Yet he had never considered the question before, and so he placed it in his heart and bowed his head. Soon a smile of gratitude came upon his lips, and he answered the boy, saying:

"There is only one moon that revolves around this Earth, yet it is a different moon for each one who sees it.

"One who never cares to look up into the night sky will never see it. For this one the moon does not exist.

"One who gazes upon its beauty only when it is full will know the moon only as a silvery disk.

"Another might view its splendor only as it rises during the harvest. For this one the moon is an immense golden ball.

"Yet another might study the moon with a telescope through all its phases, in shadow and in light. For this one it is mountains, craters and valleys, and oceans that flow with moondust.

"The answer to your question is both yes and no, for in truth is the many in one."

Yes *and* no. How could this be? Wasn't it true that things must be either one way *or* the other? Night after night the boy sat wondering, still as a stone, watching the moon travel across the starry sky.

One midnight his father found him sitting this way. "Why are you not in bed?" he demanded. "It is late. Tomorrow you'll be tired and worthless as a mosquito. Now go inside."

But the boy did not move. "Please, first tell me, Father. When you look at the moon, what do you see?"

The old man sat down and looked up into the sky. "I see the reflection of God's holy face," he said. His eyes grew soft and his voice even softer as he gazed upon his beloved moon. "I see beauty not possible for anyone but God to create, and magnificence no person or thing can ever soil. I see hope for my soul, and hope for even the soul of my son who is foolish and confuses the moon with a rock for climbing."

It was then the boy noticed that in his father's eyes two silvery crescents shown like diamonds against black seas. The sight was so beautiful, he could not look away. He stared deeper and deeper until, in the brilliance, he felt himself to be a part of their cool fire.

As though his body had drifted through the dazzling crescents' glow, he stood in the darkness from where only light can be seen. And here, seeing through his father's eyes, did he know the awe of beholding God's radiant reflection. This was not the moon he had been watching night after night, for in its milky white beams was a power more intense than the sun.

"Father," said the boy, barely above a whisper, "please hear what I say. I do not wish to make you angry, nor do I wish to feel the sorrow of knowing you do not find me worthy of your love.

"I believe you were wrong to punish me as you did, for with my eyes closed tightly against the pain, how was I able to see the truth? It is only now, when we are peaceful together, that my eyes can be open and I might learn to see more."

The boy took his father's hand and kissed it warmly with respect.

"What is this?" asked the man whose boy had become a stranger. "What has happened that my son thinks he can tell his father what is right and what is wrong?"

"Only this," said the boy whose manhood was beginning. "Tonight, without lifting a hand or shouting an angry word, you showed me what you wanted me to know. And, though I never lied to you, neither was I able to speak the whole truth, for I did not know there could be many in one.

"There is much a boy has to learn, and as a man there is much boyhood pain to forget. But tonight is a time I hope to remember for as long as I live, for tonight I was able to see with your eyes.

"And though it is true a man stepped on a far-distant stone, this also is true:

"No one walks on my father's moon."

The End
(which is also a beginning)